Dear Parents:

Congratulations! Your child is taking the first steps on an exciting journey. The destination? Independent reading!

STEP INTO READING® will help your child get there. The program offers five steps to reading success. Each step includes fun stories and colorful art or photographs. In addition to original fiction and books with favorite characters, there are Step into Reading Non-Fiction Readers, Phonics Readers and Boxed Sets, Sticker Readers, and Comic Readers—a complete literacy program with something to interest every child.

Learning to Read, Step by Step!

Ready to Read **Preschool–Kindergarten**
• big type and easy words • rhyme and rhythm • picture clues
For children who know the alphabet and are eager to begin reading.

Reading with Help **Preschool–Grade 1**
• basic vocabulary • short sentences • simple stories
For children who recognize familiar words and sound out new words with help.

Reading on Your Own **Grades 1–3**
• engaging characters • easy-to-follow plots • popular topics
For children who are ready to read on their own.

Reading Paragraphs **Grades 2–3**
• challenging vocabulary • short paragraphs • exciting stories
For newly independent readers who read simple sentences with confidence.

Ready for Chapters **Grades 2–4**
• chapters • longer paragraphs • full-color art
For children who want to take the plunge into chapter books but still like colorful pictures.

STEP INTO READING® is designed to give every child a successful reading experience. The grade levels are only guides; children will progress through the steps at their own speed, developing confidence in their reading.

Remember, a lifetime love of reading starts with a single step!

 Published in the United States by Random House Children's Books, a division of Penguin Random House LLC, 1745 Broadway, New York, NY 10019, and in Canada by Penguin Random House Canada Limited, Toronto, in conjunction with Disney Enterprises, Inc.

Step into Reading, Random House, and the Random House colophon are registered trademarks of Penguin Random House LLC.

Visit us on the Web!
rhcbooks.com

Educators and librarians, for a variety of teaching tools, visit us at RHTeachersLibrarians.com

ISBN 978-0-7364-4207-7 (trade) — ISBN 978-0-7364-9005-4 (lib. bdg.)
ISBN 978-0-7364-4208-4 (ebook)

Printed in the United States of America 10 9 8 7 6 5 4 3 2 1

Random House Children's Books supports the First Amendment and celebrates the right to read.

STEP 2 READING WITH HELP

STEP INTO READING®

Disney

WISH

THE MAGIC OF DREAMS!

adapted by Kathy McCullough
illustrated by the Disney Storybook Art Team

Random House New York

Welcome to Rosas!
This wonderful land
is known as the
kingdom of wishes.

It is a place where your dreams can come true! Here, the magical king can grant your wish.

Asha works as
a tour guide in Rosas.
She hopes to help
make wishes come true.

Valentino loves
to climb and explore.
Asha's pet goat longs
to be understood.

Sabino is Asha's
grandfather.
It is his birthday.
He is now one hundred!

Asha and her mother, Sakina, hope that the king will finally grant Sabino's wish.

Some of Asha's friends

work at the castle.

These teens serve meals

to the king and queen.

Dahlia, Gabo, Hal,
Safi, Simon, Dario,
and Bazeema all have
their own dreams.

Dahlia is Asha's best
friend and loves to bake.
Maybe she will become
the best baker in Rosas!

Bazeema likes to be
alone sometimes.
She goes to her
quiet place to dream.

Gabo can get grouchy,
but he has hopes, too.
He keeps them locked up
safely in his heart.

Simon just gave
his wish to the king.
He dreams
it will come true!

But King Magnifico
does not want
to grant every wish—
only the simple ones.

Asha used to
believe in the king.
Now she knows that
he cannot be trusted.

Asha believes that
everyone deserves the
chance to make their
own dreams come true.

She wishes on a star
for help.
The star soars
down to earth!

Star spreads stardust to let the animals speak!

They tell Asha we are
all made from stardust.
She learns that wishes
live in our hearts.

Asha tells the people
of Rosas that they
do not need magic
to grant their wishes.

Everyone in Rosas feels hope in their hearts. They are ready to make their dreams come true!

What is your wish?
What will you do
to make it real?
You have the power!